Based on the TV series *Wonder Pets!* **as seen on Nick Jr.**

First published in Great Britain in 2009 by Simon & Schuster UK Ltd
1st Floor, 222 Gray's Inn Road, London WC1X 8HB
A CBS Company

Originally published in the USA in 2008 by Simon Spotlight,
an imprint of Simon & Schuster Children's Division, New York.

A CIP catalogue record for this book is available from the British Library

ISBN: 978-1-84738-623-6

Printed in China

10 9 8 7 6 5 4 3 2 1

Visit our websites: www.simonandschuster.co.uk
www.nickjr.co.uk

WONDER PETS!

Save the Reindeer!

adapted by Tone Thyne
based on the teleplay written by Chris Nee
illustrated by Michael Scanlon, Little Airplane Productions

SIMON AND SCHUSTER/NICKELODEON

"It's Christmas eve! Let's trim the tree,"
the Wonder Pets sang happily.

But while the Wonder Pets were singing,
the tin-can phone started ringing.

"It's Santa's reindeer!" shouted Tuck.
"She's on the ice, and she looks stuck."

"This is as serious as it gets," said Ming-Ming. "Let's go, Wonder Pets!"

They built their Christmas Flyboat fast –
first the wheels, then the mast.

They hopped aboard, and off they flew –
Linny, Tuck, and Ming-Ming, too!

They sailed on through the chilly night,
and soon the North Pole was in sight!

Linny looked high and low.
"There's the reindeer down below!"

"Look – the ice is about to break...
Hurry!" said Tuck. "For Christmas's sake!"

What would our heroes use to get her?
"I know," said Ming-Ming. "Use my sweater!"

"It's teamwork time!" They gave a pull
and made a net of purple wool.

Tuck said, "Reindeer, don't be upset.
We'll save you with this purple net."

The reindeer said, "You're very nice for helping me get off the ice."

They hitched her up to Santa's sleigh
and watched the reindeer fly away.

"Now let's head back home," Linny said.
"It's Christmas eve, and it's time for bed."

Through the sky the Flyboat soared,
with three holiday heroes aboard.

Back at home, the Wonder Pets found
that Christmas cheer was all around.

Presents from Santa, a star on the tree,
and best of all . . . some celery!